Robert H. Wendover

R. H. Wendover's Views on the Monroe Doctrine

vital importance of peace, railroads, the nation's hope and blessing, and

union and fraternity

Robert H. Wendover

R. H. Wendover's Views on the Monroe Doctrine
*vital importance of peace, railroads, the nation's hope and blessing, and union and
fraternity*

ISBN/EAN: 9783337223267

Printed in Europe, USA, Canada, Australia, Japan

Cover: Foto ©Andreas Hilbeck / pixelio.de

More available books at **www.hansebooks.com**

R. H. WENDOVER'S VIEWS

ON

THE MONROE DOCTRINE,

VITAL IMPORTANCE OF PEACE, RAILROADS, THE NATION'S HOPE
AND BLESSING, AND UNION AND FRATERNITY,

WITH PRACTICAL STRICTURES ON THE

NEW CONSTITUTION OF MISSOURI.

ALSO,

A SUPPLEMENT OF ORIGINAL ITEMS OF INTEREST.

ST. LOUIS:
GEORGE KNAPP & CO., PRINTERS AND BINDERS.
1867.

R. H. WENDOVER'S

VIEWS

ON THE POLITICAL STATUS OF THE COUNTRY, ETC.

FELLOW CITIZENS : We again publish our "Views," and crave a little of your time and patience in their perusal. We have partially reviewed the past, especially since that dark picture in our history when brother contended with brother in the field of battle. But the tramp of hostile armies has ceased, and we are now endeavoring to settle down in a state of peace. Yet we deplore the loss of many thousands of our brave countrymen, who have gone to that bourne from whence no traveler has ever returned. We feel a lively sympathy for the surviving wounded soldiers who have lost a leg or arm. The conscription forced many thousands from their peaceful employments and homes, and there was no other alternative but to take up arms and war against our brothers.

At the close of the rebellion the question was agitated about engaging in another useless and unnecessary war. Some rash politicians sought the opinion of Gen. Grant, and other distinguished officers, in relation to Mexico and France. It would have been the highest degree of rashness—aye, madness itself—if our Government, at the close of our own civil strife, had intermeddled in the Mexican imbroglio, or given aid and comfort to the Fenians in their attempt to invade and occupy the Canadas. We required years of peace with all countries after our mighty struggle. The country had indeed suffered sufficiently in the sacrifice of human life, in property and treasure, and prudent and sagacious statesmen and the people were disposed to resort to all honorable means to prevent a war with any foreign power.

Since the formation of the Government we have had wars enough without engaging in any others. We had two wars with Great

Britain—one in 1776 and the other in 1812. We warred with Mexico in 1846, at the close of which Gen. Zachary Taylor, one of the great heroes of the war, was nominated for the Presidency, and elected by an overwhelming vote. Mr. Clay should have been the choice of the Whig party, rather than nominate and place in the Presidential chair a soldier who did not possess any knowledge whatever of statesmanship. At last, in 1861, the terrible civil strife began, which lasted four long years, killed and maimed for life a million of men, and after the assassination of Mr. Lincoln, Vice President Andrew Johnson became President of the United States.

The State of Tennessee has furnished three sterling, able men for the Presidential chair: Gen. Andrew. Jackson, James K. Polk, and Andrew Johnson. Kentucky had two Vice Presidents: Col. Richard M. Johnson and John C. Breckenridge, the former of whom is said to have shot the chief Tecumseh. But Kentucky had a Clay, the pride of the country, and an illustrious example of imitation among the public men of his own State which he so faithfully served and honored. A monument has been erected to his memory, at Lexington, of very beautiful proportions and one hundred and twenty feet in height.

The Monroe doctrine originated with James Monroe, one of our early Presidents, the fundamental principle of which was embraced in these few words: " No monarchical government should be established on this continent." Mr. Monroe used this language in his message: " The Government of the United States will not look with indifference upon any attempt of European governments to plant a monarchical system upon this continent." Being simply the opinion of one man, it may or may not be sound doctrine, and under unforeseen circumstances it might be inexpedient to adopt the principle. We possess sufficient territory, and so thought the distinguished statesman, Henry Clay, who expressed himself, some time before his death, against the annexation of Texas. This anti-annexation of territory was the old Whig doctrine. The occupation of the disputed territory between the Nueces and the Rio Grande inaugurated the war with Mexico. We had no right, according to the law of nations, to meddle in Mexican affairs, although it was apparent that they needed some protector or master-spirit to unite them and guide them to prosperity and happiness. We could have very readily acquired all of Mexico by peaceful negotiation, after the evacuation of the country by the French. With her mongrel population, it would have proved a source of painful regret to absorb in our body politic the descendants of negroes and Indians, and comparatively few descendants of the old Castilian or Spanish race. Neither have we any right to say that England shall not continue to hold the Canadas.

Considering the great sacrifice of human life in our recent war, and the destitution of widows and orphan children, we may form some idea of the suffering which now afflicts the country. We must consider also the enormous national debt which we are in honor bound to liquidate, by an onerous taxation which will not only burden us, but will be entailed upon our posterity and generations unborn. It is tax, tax *ad infinitum*, upon everything even down to a bill of lading and a box of matches. Is not this state of things enough to bring men to their senses? Is it not time for fanatics, abolitionists and negro worshipers to pause before forcing upon the people of the country any further extreme measures which conflict so mischievously with the conservatism and consequent peace of the country? So far as the national debt is concerned, the burden of which, as we have said, will be entailed upon future generations, we direct attention to the subjoined quotation: "Thomas Jefferson denied the power of one generation to bind another by a public debt. His opinion was, that a debt could not be contracted to extend beyond the life of the generation that incurred it."

All men are fallible, for the Bible says, "No man is perfect; no, not one." The North wished to dissolve the Union to get rid of slavery; the South wished to dissolve the Union so as to maintain the institution of slavery. So that they were both secessionists. Did you not, reader, consider an abolitionist far worse than a secessionist? Suppose the New England States were to withdraw from the Union, should they be whipped back, or should you let them go without a sigh of regret?

It was promised that if the South would only lay down their arms, this would have ended the feud, no further prosecution of the war would have been necessary, and no trial of Jefferson Davis or any of his compeers would have been required. Was this promise kept? No; the North has manifested the most unrelenting hatred for the South, and kept them out of the Union under a military government. Suppose for a moment that the South had conquered the North, are you prepared to say that, if the latter had peaceably submitted, the former would have refused to give them seats in Congress? How many good men, who are now exiles in foreign countries have lost their all upon the throw of this die! Many of the Southern men were forced by circumstances into the war without a choice in the matter, and in many instances against their own will. An unjust cause in a war, which militates against the prosperity and happiness of the people, will ever fail to meet the approval of Divine Providence.

There was considerable discussion upon the constitutional right of a State to withdraw from the Union. The question was settled in the South that ours was a mutual and conceded Union, a Union created only by common consent and interest—in fine, a contract and compact. The State of Virginia refused to go into the compact of States, at the time of the formation of the Federal Government, unless she had the right to withdraw when wronged or oppressed. Congress could make two governments if it choose, and is the only power that can declare war or make peace. Since secessionism has failed, however, I would wish all men to exert every effort to heal the great wound inflicted by our late civil war; to show charity; to forgive and forget; to let by-gones be by-gones; to "go and sin no more."

The agitation of the negro question was the leading cause of the war. Must it ever be a source of trouble to our country? The radicals have advocated the question of negro suffrage, and while the Northern States will not permit such political équality of the negro, these extreme men have forced it upon the people of the South. This political equality of the negro is insisted upon by the radicals even to an extent which would make them our rulers and masters. The Creator made a difference between us and the negro, so that he is physically and mentally the inferior of the white man; yet the unthinking and rash men in power would grant them a greater privilege than that of voting—the right to hold office and legislate for us! The ignorant and untutored blacks can very easily be instructed by their friends the radicals to claim in the South all the rights and privileges that the whites alone have heretofore enjoyed. We entertain no hostility for the negro, and wish him well personally; but they lost their happy days, good homes, and pleasant religious meetings, when they left their masters. We are all slaves more or less in this world, and the negroes, who were treated kindly by their former masters, were better off than they are at present in their enlarged state of freedom. The war might have been prevented and the country saved if the Government had purchased them. According to the Constitution they were property.

All white men, both in the North and South, if they speak their minds honestly upon the subject, are opposed to negro soldiers acting as a guard over white citizens. We believe that the negro military should be dispensed with, and that the idea is repulsive to white soldiers, especially, to mix with negro soldiers. There are naturally great dislike and prejudice entertained for an inferior race by a superior one, and an unwillingness to share in common with them, on the part of the Union soldiers during the war, in the battles and victories of the Union armies.

Mr. Clay favored gradual emancipation or colonization, and believed that either would prevent war. While they have cost us more money than they are worth, they are still among us, and it is now too late for the impoverished South and a tax-burdened country to colonize them. They would be infinitely better off were they removed to the colony of Liberia, for negroes rule in this black republic, but cannot do so permanently in this country. Since radical rule has endeavored to elevate the negro above the white men of the South, the latter possess no political rights. Should such rule continue, the families of the former white masters of the negroes will have to surrender the latter their places of nativity. Shall such outrageous wrong be imposed upon our fellow countrymen? The elections recently in the North respond in thunder tones to the question—NO!

In the South many homes have been rendered desolate, and at present a base tyranny, a military government rules the hour. During the war we had martial law in the North as well as the South; but such tyranny, through the plea of military necessity, cannot always rule among the people of the United States. In due time the people will release themselves from the yoke of a despotic Congress, when better men will take their places, the Southern States will be represented, and a return of the old days of the republic will gladden the hearts of the American people. No matter what the condition of the people has been since the war has closed, our form of government being democratic, freemen cannot long live under a military government, for the reason that they were never schooled in any other political knowledge than that which makes the people sovereign, and those who administer the affairs of government the representatives to whom the power of the people is delegated. The people's advancement in knowledge is a very great matter, and the Brazilians would prosper under a free government did they possess the enlightenment of the people of the United States. The Sumners, Stevenses, and others, are mere time-servers and creatures of the day, who will soon be forgotten, when the people generally will rise in their might and take from them the power to do further mischief to the country.

Indeed, fellow-citizens, we are heartily sick and tired of military despotism, and of seeing it prevail over civil rights and the constitutional right of representation in Congress of the Southern States. Some army officers, who are members of this military government, have become defaulters, and in most cases investigations have not been instituted, they having been allowed to enrich themselves and escape punishment. Look at the millions that have been spent at Benton barracks, and other government corrals in the United States! The lavish expenditures and peculation during and since the war are without a parallel in the history of any country.

The three distinct powers of the Government are the legislative, executive and judiciary. These are the sole legal powers which make law, neither of which ought under any circumstance to be violated. When an officer of the Government is guilty of malfeasance in office, he renders himself liable to indictment or impeachment. The people are the source of all law, the sovereign power is vested in the people, and those who administer the law are merely their agents. If a Governor violate his oath, or in any way abuse the privilege of his office, he is amenable to the law. The Governor of any State has the power to remit fines, grant pardons, and remit even his own fine; but the Legislature can impeach him, and the people can refuse to continue him in office. So far as regards the President, it is not disputed that Congress can impeach or depose him, if the charges preferred against him bear the least color of plausibility. But can they impeach Mr. Johnson on constitutional grounds? We think not, and feel satisfied that they will not attempt it, fearing the terrible consequences to the country which would inevitably result from so rash and revolutionary a procedure.

According to the Federal Constitution, no *ex post facto* law, impairing the obligations of contracts, shall be passed. Marriage, for instance, is a civil and solemn contract; but how much respect is paid to the marital law, or the marriage contract? It is often severed, and as often leaves a stain upon innocent offspring When men become bankrupt in Kentucky, some inconstant husbands among them, finding themselves in straitened circumstances, apply for divorces. Perhaps some men have made the discovery, when too late, that in electing a poor though accomplished girl as a partner for life, they have "married the whole family." Since the emancipation proclamation women have no slaves to perform the culinary duties, and their former *ennui*, the fruit of idleness and lack of exercise, has left them since they have applied themselves with alacrity to their domestic affairs. There will be fewer divorces since the wives have thus become *helpmates*.

Blackstone, in his Common Law, says, "No court can destroy a contract unless it has been violated;" nor can a contract be made null and void for goods bought and sold by individuals in any of the Northern or Southern States. How preposterous to say, when any unforeseen misunderstanding or unavoidable misfortune occurs, "Oh, I will break the contract." You may also endorse a man's note, but cannot release yourself if the other party fail to pay or curtail his note. The only remedy is to keep your name off such paper, for many good-natured, confident men, who believed other men honest because they possessed sterling honesty themselves, have been beggared by endorsing their neighbors' notes.

All should bear in mind that the Federal Constitution is our corner-stone, our chart, our beacon-light, our anchor. We cling to this great charter of our freedom as we do to the flag of the nation, and solemnly vow to protect and cherish it unimpaired under all circumstances. But should this great safeguard of our liberties ever be destroyed, the vessel of State will be stranded and sunk to rise no more. We warn you to preserve it to the end. We never wished to see the "higher law" of Northern fanatics elevated above that of the Constitution. The Bible is the great guide in our moral and religious training, but God never designed that its holy teachings should control the workings of the governments of the world. The "higher-law Bible" and the "higher-law God" doctrine is but an emanation from the brain of the mad fanatic, and not authorized by Christ, who tells us to "Render unto Cæsar the things that are Cæsar's, and unto God the things that are God's." Could these higher-law men have obeyed the teachings of the Bible, the country would not have been plunged into our late civil war, which all must concede was in a great measure the direful result of their higher-law crusade.

Stand, therefore, resolutely, my countrymen, by your noble chieftain and standard-bearer, ANDREW JOHNSON, and your conservatism and patriotism will aid our honored Chief Magistrate in bringing back to the country the good old days of prosperity and a lasting peace. Then we will revive the dear old barbecues of the past, and the parties as of yore will meet together during a

Presidential and Gubernatorial campaign and discuss again the political measures of the day. If the people had chosen a Democratic President in 1860 instead of Abraham Lincoln, we confidently assert our belief that war would not have afflicted the country with its sanguinary fields of contest, nor forced the cry of anguish from the hearts of the weeping mothers, widows and destitute orphans of the slain citizen soldiers. The mistaken policy of the people in supporting Mr. Lincoln, and the principles to which he was pledged, brought all this trouble upon the country.

So it is with individuals as well as nations, as is illustrated in the subjoined anecdote : Jesse Bledsoe, Esq., an eminent lawyer of Kentucky, once said to Henry Clay, " One misstep has almost ruined me for life. When I stepped from the window of your house, under the influence of liquor, I broke my leg, and was near breaking my neck. So it was when you voted for the Compensation Bill in Congress ; it was near ruining you." Since we cannot now recall the bitter past, let us take good heart and endeavor to repair the terrible mischiefs resulting from the mistakes or " missteps " of the extreme men in 1860, and like Mr. Clay, in his reply to Mr. Bledsoe, " Pick our flints and try it again."

Some have thought that the South would have found a better friend in Mr. Lincoln, had he lived, than in Andrew Johnson. We cannot account for the peculiarity of such persons' ideas upon this subject ; they are evidently founded upon the prejudice of the radical foes of the President. He has given sufficient evidence of his love for the people, and his efforts have been unceasingly exerted for the return of the Southern States into the Union, or their representatives into Congress, and the entire country, except the radicals, who are speedily becoming a minority party, applaud the President's policy. Even European papers recommend a feeling of kindness to be cherished and extended to the people of the South, and the suppression of all bitterness of feeling in the North as well as the South. Following the President's humane and patriotic course, the entire truly Christian communities of the North should extend the old hand of fellowship to our Southern brethren, forgetting the past and looking to the future with hope and confidence in our country. Gerrit Smith, the great abolition leader, published some time since a most able and learned address upon the necessity of extending leniency and forgiveness to the people of the South, and to assist them in repairing their losses. He quoted the Law of Nations (Vattel and other authors), and thinks the Southern people have suffered sufficiently in their great sacrifice of life and property. Wendell Phillips, another leader distinguished alike for his abolition zeal in the past, compared the situation of the South to that of a fly in a confined room, which on being safely let out of the window, was told: "Go, poor fly! I will not hurt you nor pursue you further." We need some magnanimous benefactors in the North, and the late political reaction proves that a mighty host have arisen for the relief and protection of the Southern people.

Centralization is the whole power vested in the General Government, and consolidation is the uniting of the parts of each European monarchy under one head. The people of this country want neither of these. It would be a difficult task for the President and Congress to control the State institutions and legislation of the States of the Union, and would materially conflict with the liberty of the people who have ever managed their own local State affairs. Each State is sovereign *per se*, but without the power of treating with foreign powers and levying war, which belongs only to the General Government. United together permanently by solemn compact, the States agree to support and maintain the General Government, and the latter in return protects the former in all their sovereign rights. Centralization would eventually erase all State lines, and make the sovereign States of the Union one common territory over which would be proclaimed, as in the days of the old Venitian tyranny, the edicts of a second Doge of Venice and his Council of Ten. The arbitrary measures of Congress, as far as the South is concerned, centre the powers which belong to the States, unrepresented in Congress, at Washington, and delegate these powers to commanders who reduce them to mere military orders from which the down-trodden people can make no appeal. This is centralization with a vengeance, and a despotic rule over the South which has no parallel in history. But there is a remedy for this outrage of the Radical Congress upon the liberty of freemen, and the glorious era is coming apace when the people will permanently set aside all issues which tend to distract and divide the two sections of the country, by removing all obstacles in the way of a return of the Southern representatives to Congress, their constitutional rights as sovereign States, and the exclusive control by *white* men of all their local State affairs. The great afflictions and public wrongs of a free people will eventually rebound upon the tribunal that imposed at least the latter, and this Congressional power will yet be hurled from the positions which they have dishonored, and become ever after a by-word and reproach among an indignant people.

We have hope in the future for our country, notwithstanding the present lamentable state of affairs in the South. Could we look through the vista of futurity, far beyond our own time, we might see the glorious spectacle of an augmented domain of Freedom teeming with a happy population of freemen from the Atlantic to the Pacific, and possessing a power which will defy the combined powers of Europe. We might see this noble fabric of freedom reared to its most lofty proportions by the union of hearts and the union of hands of a disenthralled and permanently united North and South. This advanced state of the free and united American people will solve the great problem of self-government, and illustrate that the government of a free people is the most sublime system on earth, supported as it will be by a people who shall be one and inseparable, a glorious brotherhood of freemen, and possessed of the power to counteract all the machinations of selfish and ambitious men. Why, then, should we be discouraged since the people of the North have recently put their fiat upon the persistent persecution and tyranny exercised over the Southern whites? It will last but for a season, and the distant epoch of the great millenium of freedom will exhibit the rich fruition of the efforts and hopes of the American patriot in these days of sadness and doubt.

We doubt the propriety and future success of the Fenian movement. It is very well for our Irish citizens to band their countrymen together, make occasional demonstrations of sympathy for their oppressed brethren in the Emerald Isle, and to relieve, with the additional aid of other citizens, the starvation and suffering of an oppressed people; but to make warlike forays upon the Canadas, and incite the people of Ireland to rebellion, will only have the effect eventually of augmenting the sufferings of their people, and of inviting a more formidable military despotism than has ruled our Southern brethren. England is too powerful in resources for Ireland, situated within such convenient reach of British iron-clads and well-trained troops, to commence their struggle for liberty. The most prosperous of our citizens, especially in our large cities, embrace a great number of Irishmen, and their condition and prospects are vastly superior to any which they could in any event have enjoyed in their native country. Under our democratic form of government our Irish fellow-citizens can enjoy those rights the exercise of which give them the most enlarged liberty of freemen. The population of Ireland has greatly decreased within the last century, and their annual emigration to this country promises an increasing exodus from old Ireland to the "land of the free and the home of the brave." Let them come by legions and become in due time absorbed in our body politic, and the future will exhibit in the green isle so many "deserted villages" for future Goldsmiths to celebrate in verse, that the census-taker will find it difficult to discover a true Irishman in a land that would teem with all the riches and plenty of a fertile soil were freedom the boon of the impulsive though generous and hospitable Irishman.

The eight-hour law movement has been agitated throughout the country for several years past. The trades-unions of the various cities have combined to lessen the hours for labor. Legislation has been resorted to, and in some instances the earnest prayers of a numerous, hard-working community have been granted. The working classes are the bone and sinew of the country, and we should protect them by every means in our power. To prevent crime in our large communities, you must make labor honorable and agreeable. Against the excessively lengthened day's toil, which prostrates and finally sacrifices so many of our best men and women, humanity calls aloud for the only remedy—two hours less for a day's labor. The health and happiness of workingmen require that a day should be divided thus: Eight hours for labor, eight hours for sleep, and eight hours to your family, country, and to God. Our own State Legislature has not been behind others in adopting this law. In addition to the eight-hour movement, a sufficient amount—say $1,000—of property and furniture should be exempt from taxation and execution, and those in moderate circumstances, especially those who compose our laboring classes, would be greatly benefitted. We should endeavor to protect by prudent legislation a numerous class of the community whose power and influence should ever demand those rights which would insure their domestic security and comfort.

STRICTURES

ON THE NEW CONSTITUTION OF MISSOURI.

FELLOW CITIZENS: The old Constitution was good enough for the citizens of Missouri. Many entertain the idea, which has some reason, that men are governed too much. Others, who would make fit tyrants to rule, conceive that it will not do to allow men too much liberty. The most enlarged liberty, when it does not conflict with the duties and rights of every good citizen, should be allowed and incorporated in every public act. The New Constitution is anti-republican in most of its features, and its illiberality is a disgrace to its framers. The clergy are even not exempt from the proscriptive requirements of this new instrument, and the test oath is demanded of them before they are allowed to exercise the right of suffrage. This test oath is the pledge all classes of men must make before they are registered voters and believed to be loyal men. Taking the test-oath was the proof of loyalty. Loyalty! The word has become so hackneyed, for the reason of its incessant repetition by men who understand so little of its true meaning, and abuse it by their anti-republican proscription of law-abiding citizens, that it grates unmusically upon the ear of every patriot and friend of his country. We want no such loyalty as that which would rule with despotic sway the white men of the South, and elevate above them the brutal and uncultured negro. Loyal citizens! The effrontery of the radicals is ridiculously apparent on public occasions when they claim such distinction, and prejudge men who have submitted to the authorities of the Government, and others who do not affiliate with this Titus Oates class politically, to be disloyal! They claim to be regarded as the only men who possess a true and thorough love for their country, while they favor all the extreme measures of the radical Congress. They claim to be the only patriots! The very men who remained snugly at home, while

brave men were battling for the government, are the select
"patriots" of the present day, who would have urged our armies
to carry fire and sword throughout the South, and hung *sans
ceremonie* every captured prisoner of war, and even those Southern
men who were not rebel soldiers, but who were *suspected* at once
of being traitors! Loyal citizens and patriots! Verily, they are
true lovers of their country—so far as a contracted and selfish
regard that their political action betrays for their own radical
friends and the negroes!

We have thus given the character of the radical persecutors
who so arrogantly take upon themselves the credit of being the
only true friends of the country. The framers of the new Constitution in Convention were the objects of the most affectionate
regard of the loyal mongers we have referred to, and fully merit
the highest encomiums of the radical Congress. To invest the
Governor of the State with an unprecedented appointing power is
in full character with these extreme men. The appointment of
some eight hundred civil officers is a stretch of power in one
man which has not to our knowledge a parallel in this country.
While we have boasted of an elective democratic government,
and contended that every office should be by ballot the free gift
of the people, this Convention declared that the people shall have
no voice in the matter, and that the one-man power shall prevail!
It made no difference, however, while the taking of the prolix
test-oath was required of every man, especially of those who were
suspected of being confederate soldiers, or aiding and abetting in
the cause. This numerous class of persons, when the new Constitution was submitted to the suffrage of the people, stayed away
from the polls, for the very sufficient reason that they did not wish
to humiliate themselves by this beggarly way of exercising a free-
man's right of suffrage. Consequently the odious new Constitution was ratified by *only* those loyal brawlers who possess so little
charity for their neighbors. Since, then, the Governor was in-
vested with this wholesale appointing power, what difference, we
repeat, if a majority of the people, who are not inclined to take
the test-oath, have not a free citizen's right to elect men of their
choice to office?

The onerous taxation which this new Constitution imposes upon
the people is without precedent. The Legislature is the proper
source which should impose taxation upon the people of the State.
This Constitution would entail its cursed incubus of taxation
upon the State for generations to come. This taxation is intended

as a permanent thing—or rather, we should say, just so long as the people of Missouri tolerate such an infamous instrument as the new Constitution. The very idea of taxing the sacred edifices dedicated to the worship of God, and invading the quiet resting places of the dead, to put a price upon the graves of the departed in the shape of taxation, is enough to horrify every true Christian in the land, and bring down the vengeance of Heaven for such sacrilegious perfidy! Might not these framers of the new Constitution as well imitate infidel France at the height of the old French revolution, and place above every graveyard, sacredly dedicated to Christian burial, "Death is an eternal sleep"? This was not near so terrible as the bare idea of exhuming the dead, if the tax upon the graves imposed by this damnable edict, in the guise of the new Constitution, were not collectable. The sectarian element is always the accompaniment of radicalism, and this *glorious* charter of the people's freedom in Missouri levies much heavier taxation upon the places of worship of the Catholic communities in the State than the Protestant places of worship! Both these religious communities are equally and justly indignant at the outrageous attempt of the framers of the new Constitution to place the heavy burden of taxation upon their places of worship. This abuse of all that is sacred, this madness of radicalism, will of course inevitably defeat itself and its purposes by such spasmodic fits of outrage and wrong upon the people, and the thunder of the people's voice will cast out the legions of devils they possess, which impel them to evil and that continually, although at the sacrifice of their political hopes and prospects. They will then become sane and of a right mind, but conscious of their past political perfidy will hide themselves from the scorn and indignation of an outraged people.

This new Constitution strikes with a parricidal hand at the private, vested rights and contracts of the citizen. The Federal Constitution says that no *ex post facto* law impairing the obligations of contracts shall be passed, and this great charter guarantees the protection of life, liberty, property, and the pursuit of happiness. But what is the use of referring to the Federal Constitution as a guide for the action of such men as the framers of the new Constitution? What is the use of directing the attention of men so confirmed in their hatred of everything liberal and enlightened? They are only keeping back the evil day—the day of retributive justice.

The incongruous features of this new instrument are so glaring that it is hardly necessary for us to adduce high authority to satisfy any one of its inconsistencies and outrageous usurpation of the rights of the citizen. We wonder very much that the Convention did not abolish the Legislature; they have considerably curtailed its powers. Why did they not say that men should not own more than five hundred acres of land, nor possess over $100,000? These constitutional framers were prepared to adopt any monstrosity that a malignant spirit would prompt them to conceive. They should have been brought to condign punishment for the wrong done their constituents by violating every principle of right and justice. The gentlemen of the Convention talked, forsooth, about treason! Why, bless you, *they* are the the most arrant traitors alive! Andrew Johnson, who has told you that all the powers of the Government are from the people, is stigmatized by such men as *traitor!* Where, then, can we find a patriot in the land? If Clay, Webster, Benton, and other well-schooled statesmen had lived, we believe there would have been no war, and consequently at its close no radicals in power to oppress with military rule the free white men of the South, and attempt to disfranchise the Democratic citizens of Missouri. How pleasant the retrospection, when we look back to the good old days of the Whig and Democratic parties! They were happy days indeed—they were the halcyon days of our prosperity, and "traitor" was a term not found in the vocabulary of either school of politicians. Those days will return—they *must* return at no distant time as certainly as there is Truth, and as surely as inspiration prompted the utterance of the immortal Jackson: "The Union must and shall be preserved."

Our learned and patriotic Attorney General, at the time the new Constitution was adopted, said it was revolutionary in its spirit, and did not meet with the approval of the enlightened citizens of Missouri. Our Governor, Thomas C. Fletcher, was opposed to it, and pronounced it "very badly got up." Opposition also came from the young and sprightly Charley Johnson, who eloquently denounced it as a sheer infringement upon the rights of the people of the State. Other persons regarded it with manifest disfavor, who were among those who withdrew from the Convention. The Turners' Hall delegation called upon the Convention demanding an adjournment of that body, and were about breaking it up by force when the military interfered. The disgustingly obnoxious features of the new Constitution were so apparent that the popular indignation was at once aroused, and had it not been for the military, who were ever called upon to protect all radical conventions in their nefarious attempts to. inflict wrong upon the citizen, the deliberations of the Convention would have been short-lived. The news was bruited about, at the time of the Turners' Hall demonstration, that the "framers" were about freeing negro property from taxation, and disfranchising the men who refused to take the test-oath. Many members of the Convention deserted it like rats from a sinking ship, and out of sixty-six members only thirty-eight signed it. No marvel that they would desert this nucleus of madmen and fanatics that signed such instrument of oppression. No wonder that sane people raised their hands in astonishment when the blow was struck at privileges granted to corporations—to bank charters, insurance companies, railroads, churches, charters to lodges, and in short disfranchised the conservative citizens of the State.

In the Presidential canvass of 1864, men were afraid to express their choice of a candidate on account of the military. Congress has since passed a law punishing any soldier or officer who inter feres in elections, yet the military are the ruling power over white men in the South at this day. The idea of men voting for the new Constitution because it possesses one good feature, is preposterous. To illustrate such absurdity and rashness, you may swallow a dozen poisonous pills for one good one, and lose your life. It would be better ten times over to reject the whole and order a new prescription. Men voted for the new Constitution because the military power was in the ascendancy, whose presence signified that they were expected to conform to the requirements of the "rule and ruin" policy of the radicals, notwithstanding the act of Congress which forbade an officer or soldier to interfere in elections. All Congressional acts will prove inoperative if they conflict with the fell purposes of the radical leaders—that is, so long as they can maintain their power, which, thank the Lord, will not be long. The reign of the old French triumvirate was short-lived, and Robespierre, who survived his sacrificed brother despots, and succeeded to the supreme power which was a reign of blood, was hurled at last to destruction by a justly indignant people. So will the dominancy of the Congressional radicals cease, if they fail to impeach the President; but if the latter suffer such ignominy, although they will eventually meet their political doom at the hands of the people, a Congressional despotism will be inaugurated of exalting still more the negroes and of further degrading the white men of the South. None could embody all the venom of fanaticism, a hatred of conservatism, and love for the negro as well as Charles Sumner, and he, like Robespierre, may aspire to the supreme power, the exercise of which would be sure to meet at last with the popular vengeance.

The cause of the revolutionary war of 1776 was oppression of the mother country. The oppressive measures of the party in power have already aroused the Northern States to peaceable political action. Let the people overthrow the ruling power in Congress, and all will be well; but should the radicals, during the residue of their terms in Congress, persist in visiting upon defenceless people unnecessary wrong and oppression, the old struggle may be resumed for the rights of man—those rights which our Federal Constitution guarantees to every law-abiding citizen of the South. We should deplore trouble like this to the country, and only speak of the possibility of such an event should the radicals be crazy enough not to heed the utterance of the people's thunder tones recently in the Northern States: Thus far shall you go, but no further! Oppression from ourselves may be borne for awhile, but the right-thinking people of the country will soon, we trust, very peaceably overthrow it. The very at- tempt of the mother country to oppress the Colonies in 1776 was resisted by our ancestors, and our liberty was achieved at last after a bloody struggle in a blaze of glory! May that flag which bears upon its broad folds the emblematic stripes of red and white, and the stars in their field of azure, awaken holy thoughts of our sacred struggle for liberty in the days of our grandsires, and we shall forget all sectional bitterness and go forth together hand in hand, brother with brother, to that goal of a perfected and ex- alted freedom which will unite us indissolubly and permanently as American freemen.

We close our thoughts upon this part of our work by directing the attention of the reader to the following from the Detroit *Tribune*, which we are proud to copy entire, reminding the reader that Hon. P. H. Wendover, "the Father of the Flag," was our ancestor:

WENDOVER, THE FATHER OF THE FLAG.

In 1778, the flag of the United States was altered at the sugges- tion of the Hon. P. H. Wendover, of New York. A return was made to the thirteen stripes, as it was anticipated that the flag would become unwieldy if a stripe were added on the admission of each State. He also proposed the arrangement of all the stars

in the Union into the form of a single star. The resolution of
1813 was as follows:

Resolved, That from and after the fourth of July, the flag of the
United States be thirteen horizontal stripes, alternate white and
red; that the Union be twenty stars white in a blue field, and
that on the admission of a new State to the Union, one star be
added to the Union of the flag, etc.

Wendover is known in history as "The Father of the Flag."
The following lines are respectfully dedicated to Mrs. Cynthia
Wendover Van Deuser, a descendant of the distinguished patriot,
and the wife of the Medical Superintendent of the Michigan Asylum for the Insane:

No wonder Wendover of old
Suggested stripes and stars of gold
 For the true standard of the free,
For when our infant nation bled,
He saw the smoking streams of red,
And the blue banners overhead,
 With the white bars of purity.

He saw the stars come gleaming through
The radiant fields of azure hue,
 A gentle hint by nature given—
To patriots pure, and brave and wise.
He copied from the glowing skies
The starry banner Nature flies,
The flag that God unfolds in Heaven.

In his descendants here we trace
A starry splendor of the face,
 Left by the light that sweetly stole
Upon his features light and fair,
From the vast worlds of beauty where
Crowned angels lean from walls of air
 To guide aright the patriot soul.

The generations yet unborn,
When they behold the streaks of morn,
 And the star-glory of the night,
Shall point with pride to one of old
Who filled our flag with stars of gold,
And underscored the blazing fold
 With the broad lines of red and white.

OF ORIGINAL ITEMS OF INTEREST.

GERRIT SMITH, unlike the bitter men who compose the Radical Congress, writes to Herschel V. Johnson in a tone which does honor to his head and heart. Mr. S. pleads in the most affecting and earnest manner for peace, for mutual forbearance, and the old return of fellowship between the two sections of the country, while neither party must claim that itself is the saint and the other the sinner. Peace he wants, as all rational men do, in which he declares that we shall then be lovingly linked together, and there will be no longer fears entertained of another breach between us, and therefore no longer doubts of our national credit and threats of repudiation.

He also thinks that the impeachment of the President, if it really should take place, would neither bring peace, nor supersede the need of it. Peace being the first need of the nation, every effort should be made to secure it. The South, convinced of the honesty and fraternal spirit of the North, would entertain the same spirit, and there would be no doubt of winning the heart of the South and bringing about a lasting peace. If Congress should at the present session appropriate FIFTY OR ONE HUNDRED MILLIONS OF DOLLARS to the war-impoverished South, for the reason that the North as well as the South was responsible for the war, an enduring peace would follow such large investment.

Mr. S. thinks, and with some reason, that if room had been given for the play of the heart in 1865, the South would have answered our loving appeals in a like spirit. The cool, cunning, calculating intellect employed by the statesmen of the country has retarded instead of hastened the reconciliation of the North and South. It is not the skill of the statesman which can so well make a lasting peace, but simply a sense of justice, and the mutual forgiveness of mutually offending brethren.

In his letter to William Lloyd Garrison, Gerrit Smith opposes confiscation and white disfranchisement. He would have the Southern leaders, whom Congress have disfranchised, allowed to vote and take part in the Government. If all the negroes in the South are allowed to vote, it is safe to accord the same right to all the whites, as the negroes could be at the polls to hold in check such whites as might be disposed to be oppressive. When the South laid down her arms, Mr. Smith thought that a temporary disfranchisement of those who had made war upon the Government would be necessary, but he afterwards believed that only a few of them should be disfranchised, and finally believed that none should be. He believes that treason is not to be charged in such a war as this, and that the conquered stand in no need of amnesty.

Mr. Smith thought at first that the large landed estates of the South should be distributed amongst her white and black poor, and that it would be a wise as well as benevolent measure; but very soon he ceased to think so. Her white poor do not call for this confiscation or distribution. As this is a war in which both parties are guilty, and neither entitled to indemnity for the past, there remains no justifiable cause for confiscation. Peace without confiscation is worth more to black and white than confiscation without peace. Poor as he is, the black man needs peace more than property, and with a return of a permanent peace he will not want property. It has been urged to distribute her soil, while a school system has been adopted for the blacks; and if the South yield to more demands, the distinction between the office of the general government and that of the State governments will eventually be obliterated, and the State governments will soon have disappeared.

Mr. S. thinks that the war arose from a mere rebellion into the dimensions of a great civil war, that Jefferson Davis should not be punished for treason, and that he should not be the target and victim, singled out from the millions in the South who sustained the Confederate government, for Northern vengeance. Mr. Davis, as President of the Confederate government, should not be pun-punished any more than those who took part with him in the rebellion. We think so too.

THE plans far building the colossal bridge across the Mississippi river to connect Illinois with St. Louis, were accepted by the Board in July, 1867. The vast importance of this great work to the entire country will strike every one who will take the least thought upon the subject. It will take three years to complete the work from the date of the commencement of operations during the summer of this year. When this mighty construction shall have been completed and ready for the transit of passengers and freight across the Father of Waters, you can take the cars from St. Louis for any place in the United States without an interruption. What a glorious achievement this great work will be for the city, and what a great impetus it will give to trade, commerce, and the increase of her population! There will be a grand Union depot constructed, from which will diverge nine different other depots centered in our city. You cannot expect a city like ours to grow in commercial importance and population without the great convenience now in progress. Building will have a fresh start, and the mechanic and laboring man can find at last permanent homes, while a sufficient number of dwellings and reduced rents will attract thousands of them to our city. Indeed all in our future populous city of some 400,000 or 500,000 souls can take the cars at this point, as we have said, for any part of the United States, and especially thousands of miles further west, when our prosperity will be at its height.

The cost of the bridge and the tunnel, without calculating the cost of real estate, is estimated at $5,000,000, the real estate being valued at $750,000. Mr. Eads, Chief Engineer, ten days after the plans of the Bridge Company were accepted by the Board, had a cofferdam constructed on this side of the river for the abutment pier. The two piers which will support the three glorious arches, spanning the St. Louis and Illinois shores of the river, will be of such immense masonry as to take back the mind involuntarily to Cheops and Cephrenes and their pyramids by the winding Nile. The mind can scarcely conceive of a grander construction of mason work, and we await its future completion for the public to view with wonder and astonishment a work of colossal magnitude that may vie with any others of modern times.

AMERICA will never be free, or happy, or united until they drive England out of the Canadas. England doubtless helped to foment the bitterness of feeling between the North and South by sending out her emissaries to distract the minds of our people. We should send out *our* emissaries to provoke and distract Old England in the same way. Some of our Irish citizens, for whose prudence we cannot vouch, have recently taken the initiative.

THE General Bankrupt Law of the United States is a wise and beneficent act. Since "this cruel war is over," one-half the people are hopelessly insolvent, and there is little chance of their ever outliving their embarrassments. This law will prove a blessing to many who can start business anew, and be again able to support their families decently. Mr. Clay mentioned in a speech, which we heard him deliver, that the old Hebrew law forgave a man his debts every seven years. We have known men, however, who would not forgive a debtor and his heirs under seventy times seven years, and, if the law could justify it, would make it incumbent upon his heirs to collect a paltry debt from the descendants of his debtor a century after date! Some of these hard-hearted creditors have radical proclivities!

THE internal revenue law—or as some ill-natured persons will call it, the "*infernal*" revenue—will tax us a hundred years to come. Loyal slaveholders should demand indemnity for their negroes hereafter. If the Government had paid them $1,000 for each of their slaves, all would have been harmony and peace in the country, and no war and taxation to alarm and burden the people of our once happy land. Internal revenue will eat out the very vitals of the present generation, and perhaps future generations to come.

IT is predicted by experienced and far-seeing persons that our young men of this day will outlive a population of one million souls in St. Louis. What a subject for contemplation! The bridge in progress over the Mississippi, and other bridges that will yet span the Father of Waters, as well as another reservoir to aid in supplying our vast city with water, will work wonders in the future.

THE right kind of reconstruction of the Southern States, and their proper admission into Congress by representation, would be a great blessing to the country. The past enmity and deadly hostility between both sections of the country, in such a case, would be forgiven and forgotten, and we could look forward to the future with abundant hope and confidence. A glorious government will arise Phœnix-like from the ashes of the past devouring flames of war; the people, enjoying the restored blessings of a free government, will cease to feel the poignancy of our grief in the loss of friends sacrificed in the sanguinary fields of our late civil strife, and we will all endeavor to outvie each other in the godlike effort to make our suffering and afflicted people in the South prosperous and happy. In the name of God and his great mercy, let all this be done, and that quickly!

'SOME persons in almost every community proclaim their wish that the national debt will be wiped out by repudiation. The war was a very rash procedure, if, as some say, it was possible to prevent it by a peaceable settlement of our national difficulties at the start. Our late bloody strife was brought on partly by want of foresight and the extraordinary lack at the time of calm deliberation and the mutual disposition of both North and South to reason together before resorting to the arbitrament of the sword. We lacked the wisdom and matured judgment which actuated the noble minds of such godlike men as Jackson, Clay, Webster, and others, who reposed in death while our fratricidal war raged in all its fury. Let us then seriously determine to become seriously united as a people, oppose repudiation by honestly resolving to pay our national debt, and we shall prosper beyond all our former hopes and expectations. We will then, like good sentinels on the watch-towers, jealously guard the fair fabric of our freedom, and defy the futile efforts of the enemies of popular government to do us harm.

OUR great statesmen had all paid the debt of nature when the war commenced. Had they lived, the people in both sections of the country, who almost deified them, might have listened to the warnings of these great oracles of the people, and not imbrued their hands in each other's blood. Well might Northern and Southern men say, who struggled against each other in the ensanguined field, like Macbeth while gazing upon his hands, "Out, damned spot!" The blood-stains shall be permanently erased when we will all unite in forgiving and forgetting the past, and a union of hearts and hands bind us together as a great brotherhood of freemen. Then will we more than ever revere the memory of such illustrious statesmen as Henry Clay, John C. Calhoun, and Daniel Webster.

THE Radical Congress of 1867 arrayed themselves against the Constitution, the Supreme Court, and the President who faithfully represents the people. Because the President has truly and honestly taken Constitutional grounds in opposition to the ruinous and tyrannical measures of the radicals, they have vainly exerted every effort to *impeach* him! The reaction that has taken place in the North points unerringly to the future when the brief reign of these fanatical constitutional patchers and negro worshipers will cease, and their iniquitous and unconstitutional measures, which are fashioned into laws, shall come under the hammer of Repeal. This revolutionary Congress is devoid of fraternity, humanity and mercy, and will be followed to their graves, when death shall have rid the country of these enemies of its peace and prosperity, by the jeers and contempt of the American people.

THERE should be in this country, as in some of the European states, an asylum erected for decayed gentlemen, which would serve as a comfortable home for the residue of their days. The friends of many of these decayed gentlemen would advance the necessary means towards the support of an institution of this character. Let all true philanthropists take the matter in hand, and we entertain little doubt that a benevolent project of this kind will be carried out to a successful termination. All business men and mechanics should have separate institutions of this sort, and with the abundant means they could command, how well would they make the last days of their superannuated brethren peaceful and devoid of all care!

SOME persons think that Louis Napoleon, Emperor of France, is the most extraordinary man in the world at the present time. The name of Napoleon, which had such magic sound during the times of the first Emperor, gave great prestige to the present Emperor, to which he chiefly owes his success and fame, and with which he has ventured to accomplish more than his distinguished uncle. We think, however, that Andrew Johnson, without the all-conquering prestige of the French Emperor—self-taught, and arriving at the pinnacle of fame as a statesman alone by his own untiring efforts—possessing the most extraordinary character in the world for firmness and decision, his manifest attachment to the people and an undying patriotism and love for his country—is the great representative man of the times, and his name will descend to posterity as the Great Defender of Constitutional Liberty.

IN the course of time many of the dwellings in our city will be dismantled and rebuilt, or remodeled. Streets and alleys will be widened, and various other public improvements, and the erection of loftier structures, will give St. Louis an appearance of elegance like that of Paris, France. The plan of Napoleon condemned whole blocks of buildings, and erected in their stead blocks of uniform height and beauty, with all the public conveniences to meet the wishes and wants of the happy Parisians. As it is with the fashions, so will it be in the future of our city when we shall have followed the Parisian style and beauty of her structures.

EVERY intelligent man should make it a rule to attend divine service at least once every Sunday. We have heard Gen. Scott say that he observed this rule most faithfully for nearly half a century. What an illustrious example for the youth of our country to follow! The old warrior never neglected this one great duty, and it is remarkable that all his other worldly or public duties were as punctiliously and faithfully observed. The prosperous and happy man, we venture to say, has not often neglected his religious duties.

HENRY CLAY uttered a truism when he said in a public speech on one occasion, that nineteen out of every twenty men did not possess common sense. Prudent men are very scarce, we all know, while reckless and unthinking men are numerous, their name being legion. The world would be more at peace and prosperous did none but prudent and sagacious men control its governments. Common sense dictates the prudence which guides us safely, if not to riches, to the goal of safety and happiness.

THE sacrifice of life and treasure during the Rebellion was terrible, and the deserted mourners as well as impoverished families of our country have suffered beyond conception the ruthless scourge of war. The national debt, as a consequence, is over three thousand millions of dollars, which will take some generations to liquidate. The Southern slaveholders, as the result of the emancipation scheme, lost from three to four thousand millions of dollars in slaves, which left them in a destitute condition. Had not the war occurred, we might well exclaim, so far as the South is concerned, Happy master, happy slave!

TO-DAY our military government costs us one hundred and twenty millions of dollars annually, yet we are not at war, and do not protect ourselves against any foreign power. Our taxes have swollen to the amount of one thousand millions of dollars annually, an impost which will compare with that of any other country. The great indebtedness of the country proves that the credit of the Government is good in the estimation of the governments of Europe, while the necessity exists of our taking many years to liquidate the national debt.

WE told President Johnson on one occasion, in 1866, that we asked the Lord to bless him in his patriotic and humane efforts to reunite the people. He replied that the prayer of the righteous man availeth much. This was a fit answer to our question, yet might have been addressed with more propriety to a churchman, or to one who does not hide his light under a bushel. We revere Christianity, and endeavor to do our duty, but lack the confidence to place ourselves in the position of "the righteous man." The prayers, however, of the patriotic throughout our country have kept our good President firm and decided, and are already promising the good days of union and harmony to the nation.

HENRY CLAY was in favor of the liberty of the press to the fullest lawful latitude, but made the press responsible for its abuse when it descends to low scurrility and defamation of character. The great Kentuckian was a high-toned man, full of enthusiasm for the cause he espoused, a profound statesman and eloquent pleader, and yet in his intercourse with his neighbors and friends, the illiterate as well as the intelligent, he was a plain, practical man. If he was ever the object of personal detraction in any newspaper, he never to our knowledge, so far as he himself was especially concerned, made the press responsible; for an acknowledgment of his merits as a statesman and patriot was cheerfully awarded by the entire press of the country, including many of the Democratic journals of his time. Detraction in some papers politically opposed to him could scarcely affect the gallant defender of the Constitution when he was conscious of having reached the goal of all his hopes and aspirations, a fame well earned, with the respect and affection of the American people.

The workingmen of his time were his most enthusiastic admirers. On one occasion, at a gathering of workingmen in one of our Eastern cities, he was called upon to address them. Mounting an elevated rostrum, he spoke in a strain of eloquence which thrilled the eager auditory, and elicited the most unbounded and rapturous applause. Pausing for a moment, he raised his hand aloft and pointed to the tall structures and spires in view, uttering in clarion tones these memorable words: "Behold your own proud handiwork—the lofty monuments erected to your own glory!" Affected as though with an electric shock, the vast multitude swayed to and fro, and one shout after another rent the air, until Mr. Clay was under the necessity, amid the continuous roar of applause, of repeatedly bowing his acknowledgments and retiring. Very few men, that have ever addressed the people, could enlist so well the eager attention of a vast multitude, and few men have lived that could move them to the same degree by his powerful reasoning and eloquence.

GREELEY astonished the country by offering himself as one of the bail for Jefferson Davis. We might call his conduct in this instance very magnanimous; yet when we consider that Davis and Greeley were as opposite to each other in politics as the antipodes, there was undoubtedly a fair opportunity for the latter to return good for evil, and thus heap coals of fire upon the head of his political foe. Greeley might also, at the time Davis was immured in Fortress Monroe, have felt disposed to exhibit not only his generosity to his old foe, but a proud superiority over the ex-Confederate President that deigned to release him from the restraints and confinement of his prison.

IT would scarcely be of any account to apply this truism to the Radicals: "To err is human, to forgive divine." They cannot see it in the light that all patriots do when they eloquently plead for a return of the Southern States and the reunion and harmony of the two great sections of the country. The solemn pledges of men, who had espoused the Confederate cause, of fealty to our Government is not sufficient with these bitter Radicals, and forgiveness is no part of their religious creed. Their prayer is not "forgive us our trespasses as we forgive those who trespass against us;" but their hostility to Southern white men will prevent them from breathing any other prayer than this: "Forgive us our trespasses, and *punish* those who trespass against us." Verily, we have a Christian Congress! Will they deserve the plaudit and welcome of Him who said: "Well done, my good and faithful servants; enter into the joys of thy Lord"? By an unceasing repentance of the past, we trust the mercy of Heaven will some day reach them!

WE once heard the celebrated negro man, Fred. Douglass, lecture. He exhibited remarkable ease of delivery, which he has so readily acquired while mingling with distinguished speakers of the superior race. Negroes ape admirably the manners of the whites, to whom they have ever looked, in their former relation of slave and master, with a kind of respect akin to reverence. Such was our impression while listening to Fred. Douglass; but his pompous account of the manner in which he was received by the nobility of England, from which country he had just returned, partook at times of the ludicrous as he waved his hand imperiously, it seemed to us, while referring to my Lord This and my Lord That. This habit of Fred, in common with others of his own race, of aping "white trash" of distinction, would enable him, if he sojourned a season in Paris, to acquire the superfluous manners of the most accomplished courtiers of the Emperor, and return to America with a *distingué* air that would astonish "white folks." Fred himself overawes without a doubt the unintellectual nigger by his grandiloquent speech; but so far as the animal is concerned, Afric's rank odor exudes from his skin on a warm summer day, and the "white trash," while Fred arrives at the peroration of his discourse, and his blood is up to fever heat, will as readily place themselves at a safe hearing distance as Sambo will approach the feet of the orator and revel in an atmosphere which bears to him the scent of the ottar of roses!

THE ground for the new Union Market House cost the city $245,000 in forty-year bonds. The cost of building amounted to $100,000, the total cost to the city being $345,000. The market building is a very great convenience to the city, and one which we could not now dispense with for a day.

The estimated cost of the Court House is $1,200,000. This is a mighty structure, and cost twenty years' labor in building. It is of colossal proportions, and occupies the space, including the railing, from Fourth to Fifth street. The rotundo is spacious and beautiful, and the stranger will be struck at once, as he views the exterior of the building, with its mighty dome, and by the grandeur of this well-proportioned and immense pile of mason-work.

The new Masonic Hall, erected by the Grand Lodge of the State of Missouri, on the corner of Seventh and Market streets, reflects great credit on the Order. This beautiful and massive structure is built of white marble, which is certaintly a great ornament to St. Louis, and puts into the shade the O'Fallon Institute adjoining it. Such structure as this will be permanent, and others that will follow it will endure for an age.

We have magnificent hotels in this city, and can vie in this respect with the best in the Eastern cities. The Southern Hotel was building some six years, and possesses every modern convenience, including the "elevator," which conveys guests and baggage from the ground floor to any altitude in the vast building. The Lindell, which was burned down last winter, possessed the same superior modern conveniences. Each of these famous structures cost about one million of dollars each.

THE test-oath in Missouri was declared nugatory, null and void, when applied to American citizens. The war is over, the rebels have submitted, and taken the most solemn pledges of faithfulness to the constituted authorities of the country, and it would be spurning the kneeling suppliant for the pardon of the President to require of him the additional pledge of the test-oath. The issue of State rights, out of which grew Southern secessionism, failed at last after a bloody contest of four years, and now we are at peace so far as hostilities are concerned, with no possibility of a renewal of civil war in the future history of our country. All are willing to return into the fold of the Union. Let them come, but let not insult be still added to injury, by requiring the test-oath as a preparatory measure for Southern men to enjoy the right of suffrage!

GEN. SHERMAN remarked in a public speech in this city, a year or more since, that St. Louis was destined to be the capital of the United States, and the second city in the Union. We must then multiply and replenish the earth, according to the Book of Genesis, invite additional emigration by reducing the rents, extend our trade and commerce, raise plentiful crops, continue to build up our great railroads, set the iron horse to work, and last, though not least, complete the St. Louis and Illinois Bridge, and we can in the future, when we shall have arrived at the destiny predicted by Gen. Sherman, reap the rich fruits of trade with the shores of the Pacific as with the Atlantic seaboard. The General recently, on the occasion of the annual festival of the Army of Tennessee, paid similar high compliments to St. Louis, and especially to the courtesy extended to him by the journals of the city and our citizens.

READER, whoever thou art, rememember to practice virtue thyself, and encourage it in others.—PATRICK HENRY.

Swear not at all, and never by Jesus Christ, the Redeemer of mankind.—JOHN QUINCY ADAMS.

Three things will always command respect in this world—talent, wealth and beauty; the opposite, ignorance, poverty, and old age, have always a downward tendency. We have known poverty, talent and uncomeliness to command almost reverence, for the possession of talent and genius made the others attractive and lovely. Charlotte Bronte, the talented authoress of some masterpieces of fiction which have enchanted the reading world, was old and poor, yet her genius made her an angel.

To YOUNG MEN we would say, be strictly temperate, join the Good Templars of Temperance, be honest, attend faithfully to your business, treat every body with a gentlemanly courtesy, and you will prosper, with a good government to protect you and yours, and under your own vine and fig-tree, where none can make you afraid, you will be happy and live a useful and honorable life to a good old age. When the sun of your life is about setting, you will enjoy the approval of a good conscience, and the plaudit and welcome of the Author of all good: "Well done, my good and faithful servants; I have been with you in the sixth tribulation, and I will not forsake you in the seventh."

YANKEE TRICKS are the lowest resort of the swindler and cheat. The Yankee will tell you a plausible story to collect a crowd, and then the misrepresentation and the lie come to get the advantage of you. After accomplishing his object, he will swindle and rob you. Both Yankee men and women practice dishonest games, whom all truthful persons should avoid. These Yankee cheats are not the true representatives of Yankeedom. We speak of the masses, and the adventurers who journey through the country to make money upon the credulity of honest people. The tricks attributed to the Yankee could just as well be played by more honest people, but who scorn deception, and would not swindle their neighbor in word or deed. Wooden hams, wooden nutmegs, and clay soap, characterize Yankee deception and Yankee swindling.

HORACE GREELEY says: "The man who pays more for his shop rent than his advertising does not know his business."

RADICALISM, which is the father of negro-ism, social-ism, true-love-ism, and spiritual-ism, characterizes the fanatical and crazy portion of the people throughout the North. But womans'-rights-ism is the most extraordinary *ism* of the day. It advocates woman's suffrage, and of course would claim as well the right to hold office. This country has got along very well without woman's suffrage, and indeed the country would elect better men to office if women never voted. It would be a great punishment to the ladies if they would place themselves in the position of the voter; but *some* of them might think it a healthful exercise to repair to the polls and jostle their male friends aside to vote ahead of them! Then the mingling of females who bear a fair reputation with the most degraded of their sex; the calm though earnest persuasion of the former to vote a particular ticket, and the noisy and profane replies of the latter who are wrangling in opposition; the rush made by the modern Xantippes to hustle away the virtuous and well informed female voters; the despoiling of head-dresses and the faces of the fair; the shrieks and cries for father, husband, brother to rescue them from the violent hands of female tigresses; the retreat of the assaulted and worsted party from the polls, and the undaunted and savage Amazons in close pursuit, while a *wide* passage is given for the parties in the chase; the repeated screams for mercy of the party pursued as they are again and again assaulted, and the triumphant yells of the attacking party; the loud laughter of vulgar men, and a general comingling of the voices of both sexes; the arrival of the police, and the arrest of good and bad among our female voters——Oh, Lord! a further picture of such probable scenes, if all women were permitted to vote, would be too soul-harrowing, and we drop the curtain! We love and respect all good women, and we believe many of them would never repair to the polls to vote; yet many of them would not only thus unsex themselves, but seek degradation by mingling with the abandoned of their sex at places of election.

GERRIT SMITH addresses a letter to Thaddeus Stevens on our duty to the people of the South. Mr. Smith says that there are two reasons why the North should be glad to help the South. First, the South is poor—very poor; and the North is rich—very rich. Second, the North is largely responsible for the poverty of the South, because our fathers united with those of the South in upholding and extending slavery. At one time every Congress was for slavery, and the Missouri Compromise was the work of the North as well as of the South. The Fugitive Slave Act was enforced vigorously. The colleges and theological seminaries generally were on the side of slavery, as well as nearly the entire people, and the commerce of the North was emphatically in the interest of slavery. Would that Congress were so just and wise as to lend fifty millions to the Southern States, to each of which so much as would be proportionate to her population, and to what she had suffered from the ravages of war. This, by proving the love and pity of the North for her, would win the South's heart, and would thus produce a true and lasting peace between them. This fifty millions, in a financial point of view, would be worth more than that to the nation.

POOR white widows and orphans, according to the last report of Gen. Miles, Assistant Commissioner of the Freedman's Bureau of North Carolina, as counted by thousands, were living on charity. There was no employment for them, and hundreds went into the fields to earn enough to sustain life, but their feeble constitutions soon broke down under the burning sun. Miserable and terrible consequences of the war, when its woes must thus be visited upon widows and orphans!

A NEPHEW of the great Henry Clay, who was stopping at the Planter's Hotel, told us on one occasion about the railroads under the French capital. For miles under Paris cars run, cattle are driven, and milk carts come out at different stations in the suburbs of the city every morning. Such a system should be adopted in the cities of this country, and thus keep our streets rid of all incumbrances, and save life and limb of the helpless pedestrian on the streets.

" How far the duty of the President to preserve, protect and defend the Constitution requires him to go in opposing an unconstitutional act of Congress, is a very serious and important question on which I have deliberated much and felt extremely anxious to reach a proper conclusion.

" A faithful and conscientious magistrate will concede very much to honest error, and something even to perverse malice, before he will endanger the public peace, and he will not adopt forcible measures, or such as might lead to force, as long as the chances which are peaceable remain open to him or to his con stituents. It is true that cases may occur in which the Executive would be compelled to stand on his rights and maintain them, regardless of consequences.

"If Congress should pass an act which is not only in palpable conflict with the Constitution, but will certainly, if carried out, produce immediate and irreparable injury to the organic structure of the Government, and if there be neither judicial remedy for the wrongs it inflicts, nor power in the people to protect themselves without the official aid of their elected defenders; if, for instance, the Legislative department should pass an act, even through all forms of law, to abolish a co-ordinate department of government—in such a case the President must take the high responsibilities of his office and save the life of the nation at all hazards."

We extract the above from the President's message, read in Congress December 3d, 1867. The language of the President is significant, and should be regarded by the people as justifiable since Congress has attempted to dispense with the Executive branch of the Government and assume the supreme power. If the worst come to the worst, and the existence of the nation be imperilled by the persistent usurpation of Congress, we believe that the duty of the President is plain, and that the people will sustain him even should he order the arrest of Sumner, Stevens & Co., those mischievous agitators and enemies of the peace of the country. Once arraigned before the proper tribunal, let justice be meted out to men who have endeavored to rob white freemen of their rights, and raised the parricidal hand at "the life of the nation." The people demand a restoration of concord and peace between the two sections of the country, and the action the President proposes to take will not only secure such blessing, but save our Government from its threatened overthrow.

During the war there were Northern men who did not appear to know the difference between municipal and international law. They clamored at first for the life of every Confederate prisoner, until taught the absolute necessity of observing the common laws of war. Since the war has closed, the trial and punishment of the leading men of the Confederate government and army have been demanded by these unthinking men, without taking into consideration the fact, that our country was actually divided into two separate states during the war, acting independently of each other, and when conquered required the same respect and consideration as any other nation with whom we were at war. Vattel says :

"But when a nation becomes divided into parties absolutely independent, and no longer acknowledging a common superior, the state is dissolved, and the war between the two stands on the same ground, in every respect, as a public war between two different nations. They decide their quarrels by arms, as two different nations would do. The obligation to observe the common laws of war towards each other is therefore absolute, indispensably binding on both parties, and the same which the laws of nations impose on all nations in transactions between state and state."

Vattel speaks as precisely of our case as though he had us only in his mind.

Hallam, Macaulay, Welker, unsurpassed authorities on such subjects, and all of our own enlightened day, fully sustain Vattel. In speaking of civil war, Hallam says :

"The vanquished are to be judged by the rules of nations, not of municipal law."

Macaulay says that, in such a case,·

"The vanquished ought to be treated according to the rules not of municipal but of international law."

THE Honololu Advertiser published an account of the discovery of land in the Arctic Ocean by Capt. Long, of the whaleship Nile. It is thought it will prove to be the polar continent. The past season was the mildest experienced by the oldest whalemen, who were enabled to reach latitude 78.30, and examined the land attentively along the entire Southern coast, and sketched its appearance. It is quite elevated in appearance, and contains near the centre, about longitude 180, what resembled an extinct volcano, which is estimated at 3,000 feet high. He named the country Urangells Land, after the Russian explorer. The west point is in latitude 70.56 north ; longitude 78.30 east. He named the cape Thomas, after a seaman who discovered it. The southeast point is named Cape Havan. The Nile sailed several days along the coast and approached within fifteen miles. The lower part of the land was free of snow, and appeared covered with vegetation. It is impossible to tell how far the land extends northward. He could see ranges of mountains in the distance.

In a speech, delivered by Hon. George Pendleton, at Madison, Wisconsin, it was asserted, from undoubted authority, that the Freedmen's Bureau and military government cost the people of our county, by appropriations and in other ways, $200,000,000! Must such lavish expenditure continue much longer? The military government controls Southern white men; the Freedmen's Bureau feeds, clothes, and teaches the negroes! Well might Sambo say, "Poor white trash!" for white men, women and children have been suffering for the very necessaries of life while lazy negroes were fed and clothed! This reign of fanatical radicalism will last but for a brief season, and the leading radicals be politically ostracized.

The taxation by the city of Cincinnati, under the Internal Revenue Law to-day, is equal to that paid by any eight of the ten States of the South. This is certainly evidence of the great wealth and consequent business enterprise of that city, and under the present adverse circumstances of the country, with her partial stagnation of trade and onerous taxation, it speaks volumes for the indomitable energy and courage of the trading men of the Queen City.

The Republican member, of Mass., Chairman of the Committee of Investigation, charged with looking into the expenditures of the Government, says, that the stealing on horse contracts, permitted by the War Department in the first year of Mr. Lincoln's administration, amounted to more than the annual expenditures of James Buchanan's administration. This is worthy of record.

The resolution for the impeachment of the President came up on the 7th of December of this year, the pending of the question being on the motion of Mr. Wilson, of Iowa, to lay the subject on the table. After considerable fillibustering, Mr. Logan said if the Chairman of the Judiciary Committee would withdraw his motion and allow a vote to be taken squarely on the impeachment resolution, the minority would withdraw all opposition. Mr. Wilson assented, and withdrew the motion to lay on the table, and moved the previous question on the resolution. The motion was seconded, the main question ordered, and the House proceeded to vote by yeas and nays on the following resolution:

Resolved, That Andrew Johnson, President of the United States, be impeached for high crimes and misdemeanors.

Yeas, 57; nays, 108.

Thus was the impeachment of the President squelched. To keep in everlasting remembrance the bitter radicals, who voted for the impeachment resolution, and who would thus have attempted to destroy the Government and brought on civil war, we append their names, which all true friends of their country will ever hold in utter detestation:

Yeas—Anderson, Arnell, Ashley, Ohio; Boutwell, Churchill, Clark, Ohio; Clarke, Kansas; Cobb, Coburn, Covode, Cullam, Donnelly, Eckly, Ely, Farnsworth, Gravelly, Harding, Higby, Hopkins, Hunter, Judd, Julian, Kelley, Kelsey, Lawrence, Ohio; Loan, Logan, Loughridge, Lynch, Maynard, McClurg, Mercer, Mullens, Myers, Newcomb, Nunn, O'Neal, Orth, Paine, Pile, Rice, Schenck, Shanks, Stevens, New Hampshire; Stevens, Pennsylvania; Stokes, Thomas, Trimble, Trowbridge, Van Horn, Missouri; Ward, Williams, Pennsylvania; Williams, Indiana; Watson, Pennsylvania—57.

THE Central Pacific Railroad expects to be able to finish their share of the trans-continental road at Fort Bridger, 120 miles beyond Salt Lake City, and if the Union Pacific Company are fortunate enough, notwithstanding Indian fights, expensive transportation, etc., to finish their end in time to meet the California branch at Fort Badger, we shall be able to whirl across the continent from the Sacramento to the Missouri in three days and a half, in two years and a half from this time.

CHRIST CHURCH (Episcopalian), situated at the corner of Locust and Thirteenth streets, fronting Lucas Park, will be a very stately and elegant edifice when fully completed, and will cost $300,000. It will be among the most attractive church buildings in St. Louis.

The Jewish Synagogue, situated on the corner of Seventeenth and Pine streets, is a very handsome structure, and the probable cost is from $50,000 to $75,000.

THE debt of the United States amounts to $3.000,000,000, $2,200,000,000 being in liquidation form, bearing interest.

SINCE the impeachment of the President has been squelched, there is some talk of arresting Ashley, who originated the ridiculous farce of impeaching our patriotic Chief Magistrate, and arraigning him for suborning witnesses to testify against the President for his "high crimes and misdemeanors." Such men as this Ashley richly merit punishment; but the greatest punishment which he can endure for life will be the scorn and execration of a justly indignant people.

IMPEACHMENT is an accusation or charge brought against a public officer for maladministration in his office. In Great Britain it is the privilege or right of the House of Commons to impeach, and the right of the House of Lords to try and determine impeachments. In the United States, it is the right of the House of Representatives to impeach, and of the Senate to try and determine impeachments. In Great Britain the House of Peers, and in the United States the Senate, and the Senates of the several States, are the high courts of impeachment.

ON the 9th of December, 1867, three prominent citizens of St. Louis departed this life. Edward William Johnston, a literary man of considerable celebrity, died at his residence in Dayton street, after an illness of over four months, aged sixty-eight years. He was a brother of Gen. Joseph E. Johnston.

Dr. Stephen W. Adreon, an old physician of the city, and in past years a member of the Council, died at his residence, No. 1311 North Fourteenth street. At the time of his death he was Seventh ward physician and a member of the Board of Managers of the House of Refuge. He possessed some excellent personal traits, which won the esteem and respect of the community.

Edgar Ames, one of our wealthiest and most public spirited citizens, died at his residence at Sixteenth street and Washington avenue. He was a young man in the prime of life, and his death occasioned deep regret in the community. He was widely known as a prominent member of the house of Henry Ames & Co., of Main street, and as an heir and manager of the Lindell estate.

HENRY CLAY for some years, while he was member of Congress, wore blue home-spun Kentucky jeans, until at last, when his great public services won him friends and admirers, some of them presented him occasionally with a suit of fine black American cloth, which he donned with great pleasure.

IT is a fact not generally known, especially in the East, that the German population of St. Louis is 80,000. They are generally an honest, law-abiding, industrious people, and deserve well the success resulting from their efforts to accumulate property.

TEMPERANCE.

What has ruined the hope and vigor of youth,
And wrecked all the worth and honor of manhood?
What has barbed the shafts of disease,
And opened the fountains of crime?
What fills our asylums with paupers,
And strews earth with unhonored graves?
What peoples our cities with mourners,
And opens the gulfs of despair?
INTEMPERANCE.

What makes age keep the promise of youth?
What brings plenty in poverty's train?
Gives health where avenging disease
Has laid the wan blight of its hand?
What gladdens the sorrowing wife?
Brings bread to the famishing child?
Raises men from dishonor and vice,
And to sorrow, and want, and despair,
Comes to light up the darkness of earth
With the brightness and blessing of heaven?
THE TEMPERANCE PLEDGE!